The Magnificent Tree

By Nick Bland and

Stephen Michael King

Scholastic Canada Ltd.
Toronto New York London Auckland Sydney
Mexico City New Delhi Hong Kong Buenos Aires

For Ana Vivas and her new adventure   NB
For fun   SMK

Scholastic Canada Ltd.
604 King Street West, Toronto, Ontario M5V 1E1, Canada

Scholastic Inc.
557 Broadway, New York, NY 10012, USA

Scholastic Australia Pty Limited
PO Box 579, Gosford, NSW 2250, Australia

Scholastic New Zealand Limited
Private Bag 94407, Botany, Manukau 2163, New Zealand

Scholastic Children's Books
Euston House, 24 Eversholt Street, London NW1 1DB, UK

Library and Archives Canada Cataloguing in Publication
Bland, Nick, 1973–
    The magnificent tree / Nick Bland ; illustrated by Stephen Michael
King.
ISBN 978-1-4431-1962-7 (bound).--ISBN 978-1-4431-1963-4 (pbk.)
    I. King, Stephen Michael II. Title.
PZ7.B557Mag 2013   j823'.92   C2012-904747-3

First published by Scholastic Australia in 2012.
This edition published by Scholastic Canada Ltd. in 2013.
Text copyright © Nick Bland, 2012.
Illustrations copyright © Stephen Michael King, 2012.

6 5 4 3 2 1   Printed in Malaysia 46   13 14 15 16 17

Bonny and Pop were always bursting with ideas.

Pop liked Bonny's ideas

   because they were simple, clever

and properly made.

Bonny liked Pop's ideas because
they were big, brave and brilliant

with bits sticking out.

Between them,
they had ideas for just about everything.

Everything, that is . . .

but the birds.

Bonny and Pop loved the birds and wished they could stay.

and away.

and over...

over...

But every day the birds flew

"What we need is a tree!" said Bonny.

"I completely agree," said Pop.

And they both knew exactly how to make one.

Pop's idea was big and brave.

His idea was so big it couldn't fit in his head all at once.

He had to write it down and draw pictures
of it so it wouldn't get away.

Bonny's idea was simple

and it fit right there in

the palm of her hand.

They tinkered through summer,

and toiled through autumn.

They sawed, hammered and built

their way through winter . . .

Bonny and Pop enjoyed every day they spent together.

And on the first day of spring
Pop's tree was ready.

Just in time for the birds.

They filled the air with feathers and song
and flew all around Pop's brilliant tree.

Then they landed in the branches of the little orange blossom . . .

simple, clever
   and properly made.

"What a magnificent idea,"
said Pop.

"Perfect," said Bonny. "Just perfect."